GREENAPPLE STREET BLUES

Greenapple Street Blues

Ted Staunton

Kids Can Press Ltd.
Toronto

Kids Can Press Ltd. acknowledges with appreciation
the assistance of the Canada Council
and the Ontario Arts Council
in the production of this book.

Canadian Cataloguing in Publication Data

Staunton, Ted, 1956–
  Greenapple Street blues

ISBN 0-921103-15-8

I. Title.

PS8587.T38G73 1987   jC813'.54   C87-094244-1
PZ7.S72Gr 1987

Printed and bound in Canada
Typeset by Alphabets
Cover Design by N.R. Jackson

Kids Can Press Ltd., Toronto

87 0 9 8 7 6 5 4 3

Contents

For Brian Etienne, Ginny, Joyce, Margie,
Mike, Ricky, Rob, Valerie, and,
as always,
Melanie, Mom and Dad.

What's New?

"**Y**our socks don't match, Cyril."
We were walking down Greenapple Street to school on Monday when Maggie told me that. I looked, then I groaned. Maggie was right again, one sock was green and the other was blue. It was the perfect beginning for a rotten day.

Maggie said, "Sorry, Cyril, but they look silly and geniuses like me notice things like that. Don't worry, nobody else will."

I wasn't so sure, but I didn't feel like arguing with a girl smart enough to be called the Greenapple Street Genius. Instead I tried to explain: "I was in a big hurry. My mom went to work again this morning."

"Neat," said Maggie. "That means you'll be coming to my house for lunch."

I had forgotten about lunch. I had to go to Maggie's at noon on the days when my mom went to work as a substitute teacher. She had just started but she called it "going back to work" because she was a teacher before I was born.

"Your mom must be a good substitute teacher," Maggie said. "She sure is busy."

It was only the third week of school and my mom had worked four times already. "I guess," I mumbled. I could not imagine my mom being any kind of teacher at all, plus I was grumpy about my socks and I liked going home for lunch better than going to Maggie's.

I thought the day was terrible already, but then it got worse. Maggie started in on her favourite topic: the baby her mom was expecting. "My parents are whispering about it, Cyril, I know it," she said urgently. "Have you heard anything yet?"

"No," I sighed. Maggie's mom had gone to the hospital to have some test that told her if the baby was going to be a boy or a girl. The problem was, Maggie's mom wouldn't tell Maggie. She said Maggie wasn't the only one who liked surprising people.

So Maggie had gotten me to be a spy. I was supposed to listen and report if my mom talked to Maggie's mom. If I found out about the baby Maggie was going to give me a big reward—she wouldn't say what. Spying had been fun for about a week, then it got pretty dull because I never found out anything. Still, Maggie kept bugging me about it. And what made it really bad was there were still four whole months to go before the baby arrived.

"Are you sure you're trying your best?" she asked suspiciously.

"Yeah," I scowled.

"Well, just make sure. This is important, you know. They're whispering about something and I have to know if it's about my brother." Maggie didn't know the baby was going to be a boy, but she was just dying for a baby brother. Don't ask me why.

"You're going to have to do better if you want that reward, Cyril," Maggie said, pointing a finger at me.

Bossy, bossy, bossy, I thought, gritting my teeth. Socks and baby brothers; Maggie just had to be right all the time. And she had to let you know it.

I looked for a stone to kick and couldn't find one. These days everything seemed different. Well, not everything, but a lot and it bugged me. If my mom weren't a substitute teacher, then my socks wouldn't be mixed up and I'd be going home for lunch, like before. And I was tired of hearing about babies, too. I tried to think about school instead. School might be dumb sometimes, but at least you knew what to expect. Mr. Flynn was our teacher again this year because he changed grades with us. I imagined him standing at the front of the class telling us funny things and twirling his big brown moustache till it nearly poked him in the eye.

When we got to school, Maggie went down the hall to the library and I went right to Room 7, our room. The lights were on and the room was empty except for a stranger at the bulletin board. He was pinning up big letters that spelled out WHAT'S NEW? I started to sneak out but when the stranger said, "You win the early bird contest, Cyril," I stopped dead. The voice sounded like Mr. Flynn. I looked closer. The stranger laughed. Then I understood: The stranger *was* Mr. Flynn. He had shaved off his moustache! I was so surprised that my toes scrunched up in my shoes.

By the time the bell rang everyone was talking about the new Mr. Flynn. Bobby Devlin was pretending to shave with his ruler. Monica Goodman was gabbing to everybody out in the hall. I just sat at my desk and stared. The new Mr. Flynn looked awful. His mouth was so little it was as if he had no lips at all. When he had his moustache you couldn't see his lips, but at least you figured they were there.

After opening exercises Mr. Flynn went to twirl his moustache the way he always did when he had an announcement, then put his hand down, kind of embarrassed. "Okay, everybody," he said, "as you see there is something new about me today. I have shaved off my moustache."

"How come, sir?" called out Bobby.

"It was time for a change," said Mr. Flynn. His face got red and he laughed a little bit. "My wife said she couldn't remember what I looked like without it and neither could I."

"Are you going to grow it back?" George asked.

Mr. Flynn shrugged, then straightened up. "I haven't made up my mind yet, George. Now, the reason—"

"But it looked so neat," Lester said.

"Yeah," said a whole bunch of us, all boys. Mr. Flynn looked surprised.

Then Monica said, "Oh, but sir, now you look like Lance Sharpe on *Sharpe Edges* on TV. Stay this way, pleeeeease?"

Now Mr. Flynn looked really embarrassed. All the girls giggled. All the boys groaned. Girls always drooled about Lance Sharpe because they said he was cute. All the boys knew *Sharpe Edges* was the dumbest show on TV. Not even Lance's talking dog was funny.

Mr. Flynn said, "I'll think about it and I'll keep your comments in mind. Now, I was about to say, here's something else that's new." Then he told us about the WHAT'S NEW? bulletin board and how we could put stuff up about current events and things that happened to us and start the day by sharing it all.

"Does anybody have anything they want to share with us this morning—besides my moustache?" asked Mr. Flynn.

Bobby put up his hand. "Cyril's socks don't match," he said.

At recess everybody but Maggie was talking about the moustache. All the boys wanted it back and all the girls didn't.

For me this was the last straw. I climbed up on the jungle gym and said to the boys, "We have to help him make up his mind. He's just not Mr. Flynn without it."

"How are we going to do that?" said George.

"Easy," I said. "We get Maggie to make a plan." Maggie and I always did stuff like this, together. We were partners.

Bobby said, "No way, she'll wreck it, she's a girl."

We had to waste most of recess arguing with him. When he finally gave in and we ran to Maggie, it was too late: the girls were already there.

"Hey," I said to Maggie, "we're supposed to be partners."

Maggie shook her head. "This is business, Cyril.

14

I don't care about silly moustaches myself, but it's a nice little problem for a hired brain, and since the girls asked me first I'm working for them, and as long as they do everything I say...." She looked around. The girls all nodded.

"Oh, yeah? Well, who needs you anyway?" said Bobby.

"Good question." Maggie smiled. "Why don't we have a bet to find out? If Mr. Flynn grows the moustache back, the boys win. If it stays off, the girls win. The winners get to be bosses in the schoolyard for a month."

Alarm bells clanged in my head. No way, I thought, no bets with Maggie; you never bet with the Greenapple Street Genius.

Before I could say anything, Bobby snapped: "No problem! We'll cream you. C'mon, you guys." The girls laughed as we walked away.

"What do we do now?" I moaned. I felt like a bug waiting to get squished.

"I dunno," said Bobby, "but you better think of something fast, because it was all your idea in the first place."

"Huh?"

"Yeah, c'mon, Cyril," said Lester, "you always hang around with Maggie. Think of something."

"Well..." I took a chance, "if I come up with a plan, you have to do anything I say!"

"Sure," George said, "just win the bet. We

15

don't want any girls bossing us."

"Right," I said, as the bell rang. It was me against Maggie. All I had to do now was think of something brilliant.

At lunchtime Maggie wouldn't talk about the bet. When we got back to the schoolyard she went off with the girls and I sat down by myself near the doors to think. Around the corner I heard two teachers laughing and talking about Mr. Flynn and how he looked like a kid without his moustache. "He's making me feel old," one said. "Maybe we should get up a petition for him to grow it back," said the other. I didn't know what a petition was but it sounded good. I was rounding up the boys before the two teachers had finished chuckling.

"Tomorrow," I said, "we are going to make a petition. You guys have to keep this a secret until then." That would give me time to figure out about petitions. Everybody cheered and slapped hands and told me way-to-go. I felt excellent —until I saw spying Monica sneak away from us and right over to Maggie.

After school I fidgeted at Maggie's. I couldn't ask *her* about petitions, that was for sure. She spent the whole time writing something on a long piece of paper. When I asked what it was she said it was secret. I chewed my fingernails till my mom got home.

At dinner that night when my mom said she was going to work again tomorrow, I hardly noticed. I even forgot to complain about my socks. What I wanted to know about was petitions.

"It's a way of asking for something," my dad said. "You write what you want on a big piece of paper and get people to sign it to show how many people agree. Then you give it to the person you're asking." My dad is pretty smart about stuff like that.

I told them all about the moustache, except for the bet.

"Do you think Mr. Flynn will want to get a petition?" my mom asked. "After all, it's his moustache."

"Sure," I said, "he's keeping our comments in mind."

"Well, just take it easy," said my dad. "I remember how I got teased when I shaved my beard off once."

"You shaved off your beard?" I was amazed. I couldn't imagine my dad without his beard. Even when he talked about being a kid I pictured him with a hairy face, only littler.

My dad said, "Yup. When you were born. We thought it might scare you."

"Oh." I hated hearing stuff about when I was little, especially cute stuff. "Are you going to shave it again?"

17

"Nope," said my dad. "At least, not right now, anyway." Did that mean sometime? I didn't have time to worry about it right now.

After dinner I got a piece of paper and printed at the top: PLEASE GET BACK YOUR MUSTACH. IT LOOK NEAT. I wrote my name in pen underneath and the petition was ready.

The next morning I went to school early and got all the boys to sign up. Then I gave our petition to Bobby and told him what to do. Across the schoolyard Maggie was doing something with the girls, but I was too busy to see what it was.

As soon as Mr. Flynn asked, "What's new for today?", Bobby's hand shot up. He said, "Sir, we want to give you this petition from all us boys to get your moustache back. It's got thirteen names!" He handed it in and all the boys clapped like crazy.

Before Mr. Flynn could say anything, up jumped Monica, who gave him a petition from the girls to keep his moustache off! The girls all cheered. Theirs had fourteen names.

Mr. Flynn pinned the two petitions on the bulletin board. "Well," he said in a puzzled kind of voice, "thank you very much. I'll think about these but I'm not sure they'll help. You see, they're just about even and I want to please myself, too. Now, is there anything new besides moustaches?" There wasn't, so it was time for arithmetic.

As we opened our books I whispered to Maggie, "You cheated! That was my idea."

Maggie just gave me a big smile. Then she licked her finger and pretended to score on her desk. "One for me, Cyril," she said.

Now I was mad. I planned all through arithmetic and spelling and by recess I knew exactly what to do: I sent Lester to spy on Maggie and the girls.

He came back just before the bell and told us that they were going to buy a Lance Sharpe poster for Mr. Flynn to show him how he looked now. We needed a poster of somebody with a moustache. Nobody could think of anyone, so at last I said, "Everybody bring as many pictures as you can of guys with moustaches. We'll stick them together and make our own poster."

The next morning we hid in the washroom and pasted all the pictures together, even a couple where we had to draw moustaches on with marker pens. I folded up the poster and gave it to Lester to hide in his shirt.

This time we let the girls go first. When Mr. Flynn asked, "What's new?", Karina made a little speech and gave Mr. Flynn the Lance Sharpe poster. The girls oohed and aahed. It nearly made me sick. Mr. Flynn didn't look like that at all, and he never unbuttoned his shirt. I gave Lester the signal.

"Sir!" he called. "We have a poster, too! It's of, of—" Lester was having trouble pulling out the poster. There was a ripping sound and out it came, except the half that stuck to his shirt. Mr. Flynn helped him unfold it and put it back together. "That's a lot of glue, guys," he said, wiping his hands.

The posters went up with the petitions. Ours was bigger.

Mr. Flynn thanked us and said he was glad we were interested in his moustache. "But," he said, "I'm getting a little tired of hearing about it. And nobody has given me a real reason to grow it back or keep it off. Now, is anything else new?"

Nothing else was. As we opened our readers, I snickered, "Even," at Maggie and scored one on my desk. But instead of getting mad she reached over and patted my arm. "Don't worry," she whispered, "I'll finish you off tomorrow."

Silent Reading wasn't easy after that. I shifted in my seat as awful pictures of girls bossing us around the schoolyard paraded through my brain, followed by pictures of all the boys killing me because I blew it. I figured I had one more chance. But what was left to do? Then I remembered: reasons. Mr. Flynn wanted real reasons. As the idea grew I peeked at Maggie and saw her peeking at me. We both looked away fast. I knew there was no time to lose.

There was a lot to do: thinking, drawing, cutting, taping, printing, and practising. Bobby said he had to do the talking for us to win. "And we better win," he said, glaring at me. A prickly feeling ran down my back. Bobby got to do the talking. Lester and George got to carry the sign. Everybody else got to be a thumper.

The next morning Maggie and I each had a bagful of stuff to take to school. When we got there, she said, "Say your prayers, Cyril" and ran over to the girls. I went to the classroom feeling as if the bones had fallen out of my body.

Room 7 filled early that morning. Everybody knew this was the showdown. All you could hear were whispers and shuffling as things got hidden in desks and stuffed in pockets. I sat at my desk and thought the plan over and over. It had to work. It *would* work, but still. . .what was Maggie up to?

The PA came on and I jumped up. The anthem. The Lord's prayer. We sat down. The announcements. Then Mr. Flynn asked, "What's new?"

The girls waited. The boys held their breath. I counted to ten and thumped. All the boys began to thump their desks with one hand. With the other they took out big brown paper moustaches and put them on. George and Lester leaped up to

the front and unrolled a huge sign. The thumping
stopped. Bobby stood up and began to read what
we had written on the sign.

REASONS FOR MUSTACHS
Keeps lips warm
Keeps nose warm if you brush it up
Less face to wash
Makes you look happy or mad
Holds extra food
Looks tough
Saves you from kissing
GET ONE TODAY!!!!

The guys all cheered. Then the room grew quiet
again as we waited for the girls. I was almost too
scared to breathe.

At the exact second I couldn't wait any longer,
Maggie said, "Now." Out of a desk came a little
tape recorder. Marching band music started to
play. The girls stood up, marched in place and
took out big red paper lips and put them on. Sara
and Karina ran to the front with a bigger sign and
stuck it in front of ours. When the music stopped
Monica read:

CLEAN IS KEEN. NO MUSTACHE MEANS
Cool face in summer
No icicles in winter
Cleaner face washes
Crumbs don't stick
Looking famus and hansome
Easier kissing.
SHAVE AND LOOK SHARPE!

The music played again while the girls sat down. Then the room was still. I wanted to moan out loud. Maggie had done it again; the boys had lost for sure.

Mr. Flynn pinned up both signs. He thanked us for our trouble, and said we had great imaginations, super ideas, and that. . .it was time for arithmetic. Everybody groaned. It was like opening a present and finding an empty box. Mr. Flynn had to say *something*. But he didn't—until recess, that is. Then he asked Maggie and me to wait behind. My stomach did a somersault.

We sat there as the classroom emptied. The room grew very still. I felt the palms of my hands getting sweaty as Mr. Flynn shuffled the papers on his desk. You could hear every little sound. Finally Mr. Flynn stood up. As he came over I looked at Maggie, fast. She didn't seem bugged at all.

Mr. Flynn perched on a desk in front of us. I stared at his knee; I didn't want to see his face right then. "First of all," he said, "congratulations on your great ideas. They are your ideas?"

I peeked up; he was looking at both of us, instead of just at Maggie. That was something new; I sat up a little straighter.

Mr. Flynn went on. "Next, I want to ask you why my moustache is such a big deal. Cyril?"

All at once my brain shut off. What was I supposed to say? I couldn't say it was because now he looked funny or because I didn't like mixed-up socks or even that I just wanted things like they were before; it all sounded too dumb. I looked down again and mumbled, "I don't know. Now it's different."

"But I'm still me," said Mr. Flynn. "It doesn't matter what I look like, does it?"

Sure it did. Mr. Flynn didn't understand at all and I knew I could never explain. I got a sinking feeling that I would get into more trouble if I said any more, so I said the only thing I could think of to get out of the whole mess. "It doesn't matter to me, sir. I'm just a hired brain for this bet we have."

Maggie's head snapped around. "Wha-uh, me too," she said.

"And just what is this bet?" asked Mr. Flynn.

It sounded pretty goofy when I told him.

"Well," he said, "maybe you'd better put those hired brains to work on another problem. You see, no matter what I do now, half the class is going to be mad about it, and everybody will end up unhappy, including me. You got me into this mess, you get me out."

I almost moaned out loud, but Maggie started making suggestions right away. "Half a moustache, a moustache for half a year, flip a coin, bribe half the class, a fake moustache every other day—"

"No, no, no," said Mr. Flynn to every idea. While he told us why they wouldn't work, I just sat there listening. I didn't have a clue. You either had a moustache or you didn't, that was all. I mean, what else was there? Because of the bet, it was even worse than if my dad had shaved his beard again. Or maybe beards were just different. Well, they *were* different. After all, they made you—Wait a minute. Like my. . .shaved his. . .different. . ."Hey," I yelled, "you can grow a beard! Then it's a tie. Nobody wins 'cause you'd be different!"

Maggie and Mr. Flynn stopped talking and looked at me. I felt my face get hot and wished I hadn't yelled something so silly.

"Or," Mr. Flynn said slowly, "everybody wins because nobody loses. I think I like it! If you can keep this a secret I'll tell everybody tomorrow for

What's New." He smiled and rubbed his face. "Thank you, Cyril. You know, I've never had a beard. I wonder how I'll look."

"Different," I suggested, but different suddenly didn't seem so bad after all.

As we went down the hall Maggie said, "Great idea, Cyril. I was going to think of that next myself." She sighed. "It's too bad about the bet, though. I was really going to make Bobby work. But, maybe it's good it's a tie. Now we can be partners again."

"We'll be unbeatable," I said. I felt about ten feet tall.

"Completely terrific," said Maggie. "Let's shake."

We went outside, partners again.

We kept the secret of the beard until the next day when Mr. Flynn told everybody. I thought they'd guess because his face looked dirty where he hadn't shaved, but he surprised them all, especially when he said that if anybody was betting on this he guessed it was a tie. It was perfect—almost.

The only thing missing was Maggie. When I called for her that morning, her mom had told me not to wait, and she didn't come into class until Mr. Flynn was almost done.

I signalled her as she sat down but she stared straight ahead. Her eyes looked funny, kind of watery and red. Maybe she's sick, I thought. Then when Mr. Flynn finished and asked if anything else was new, Maggie put up her hand. I smiled. I didn't want to start school work yet.

Maggie stood up and announced, "I'm moving."

Fair Shares

At first I didn't get it, but when Mr. Flynn shushed everybody and asked, "Where are you moving to, Maggie?" I understood. It felt as if a basketball had hit me in the stomach.

Maggie said, "We don't know. Across the city, maybe. As soon as we sell our house and buy a new one." Her voice sounded shaky.

"That's big news," said Mr. Flynn. "Moving can be really exciting. I hope you'll be here to share that with us for a while yet. Thanks for telling us."

The rest of the morning was a mess. Maggie on the other side of the city! She might as well be a million miles away. And when was she moving? Today was Friday; would she still be here Monday? I tried to do my work but every time the thought of Greenapple Street without Maggie

28

sneaked across my mind, the basketball plopped into my middle again.

"But how come you're moving?" I asked as we went slowly up Greenapple Street at lunchtime. I didn't feel very hungry.

Maggie groaned. "The building where my dad has his dentist office is closing and he couldn't find a new place. So he wants to buy a big house and put his office at home. There might not have been room for us all here anyway, once the Junior Partner arrives." The Junior Partner was what they called the baby that was coming. For once Maggie didn't sound excited about it.

"But you can't just move," I said. "We have to do something!"

"I know, I'm working on it." She didn't sound very hopeful. I crossed my fingers and tried to cross my toes, but deep down I didn't think even Maggie could fix this mess. As we went up the driveway she stuck out her tongue at the For Sale sign on the front lawn.

Maggie's mom gave us my favourite tuna sandwiches for lunch. Maggie grumped that there was too much mayonnaise on them. Her mom said no there wasn't and asked us how would we like to go to the fall fair in the country tomorrow. I said I'd ask my parents. A fair sounded neat, and if we were all at the fair Maggie couldn't move on Saturday. I began to feel a bit better, but Maggie just sniffed, "Why tomorrow?"

Maggie's mom poured herself some tea. "Saturday is the day for fairs," she said, "and the lady from the real estate office wants to have what they call an 'open house' here tomorrow. We'll go out for the afternoon and she'll stay to show the house to people who come to look. Maybe somebody will like it enough to buy it." Maggie's mom smiled at us. We both looked down at our sandwiches.

"Well, my room is out of bounds," Maggie announced. "I've got my toad collection in there."

"There's no out of bounds, young lady," said Maggie's mom. "And dishes in the sink, please. The Junior Partner and I need a little rest. Tonight we're all pitching in to get this place tidy."

That night my parents said it was okay for me to go to the fair, so after lunch on Saturday Maggie and her parents and I piled into their car and took off. The real estate lady waved goodbye. I didn't like her. She kept calling me sweetie.

It took way over an hour to leave the city and get to this town called Grandville. At first Maggie was cross.

"I had a plan," she whispered. "I tried to mess up the house instead of tidy it, but they caught me. Then they took down my 'out of order' sign in the bathroom. They even made me take my toads out to the garden. I only got Elmer and Ugly Augie back inside.''

I shuddered. Ugly Augie was the biggest, ugliest toad I had ever seen. He was named after Ugly Augie Crumley, a bully at school. If you were only going to have one toad, it better be the creepiest one. Still, I could see why Maggie was mad.

But as we got closer to Grandville she cheered up. We watched license plates and played I Spy. Except for the leaves changing colour it felt just like summer, and moving from Greenapple Street seemed a long way off compared with an afternoon at a fair.

Big signs pointed the way through Grandville to the fair. The parking lot was a field. We left the car and walked over to the entrance gate where Maggie's dad bought tickets for all of us. Right away Maggie started begging for us to go around on our own, like the other kids we saw all over the place.

"Okay," said her mom, "I don't think you can get lost at a small fair like this one. Meet us back here at the gate at three o'clock sharp. And don't leave the fairgrounds.''

Maggie set her watch so the beeper would go off at the right time and we took off into the fair.

We ran for a bit, then started walking through the crowd. I wanted to be everywhere at once and do everything right now.

The air was full of music from the rides, and screams, and the clacking of game boards and people yelling, "Step right up," and engines, and loudspeaker voices, and laughing and talking, and through it all floated the smell of french fries with vinegar and ketchup. It felt like the most exciting thing that could happen to you might happen if you just walked in the right direction. All you had to do was decide which way to go.

Maggie made us walk all the way around once to see everything. It seemed as if there were a million things, but it didn't take too long. We ended up at a big orange building called the Pumpkin Palace. Inside were fruits and vegetables, and pies and cakes, and pictures and quilts and knitting—all kinds of things that had won prizes for best at the fair. At one end was a stage with drums and microphones for a band on it. Next door was another building that had farm animals.

Maggie counted our money. We had enough between us to go on two rides, split some french fries and play one game each, with fifty-two cents left over. Then we could look around in the Pumpkin Palace for free and visit the animals.

"Rides first," Maggie said, but on the way I spotted something else. At the door of the Pumpkin Palace was a sign that read:

!!! BIKE RAFFLE !!!

WIN THIS OFF-ROAD ACTION BIKE FROM
STEVE'S SPORTS!
TICKETS 50¢
ALL PROCEEDS TO GRANDVILLE MINOR
HOCKEY ASSOCIATION.

Beside the sign was the most perfect bike I had ever seen. It was jet black with low, gleaming handlebars and handbrakes, big knobbly tires and bright yellow wheels.

"What a bike!" breathed Maggie.

I nodded and said, "Let's get tickets."

"We can't," Maggie said. "We don't have enough money. We'd have to give up something else."

We stood there looking at the bike and wishing. "Unless," Maggie said slowly, "we took our. . . I've got a plan, Cyril. We're going to make a deal. We use our leftover money and buy one ticket. That means we have to share it. When we win we both own the bike. And that means that I can't move and take the bike and you can't keep it either. They'll have to let us stick together and share!''

I thought hard. "We'd have to prove it," I said, "or nobody will believe us."

"Good thinking," said Maggie. "I'll write it down and we'll sign our names. Then it's a deal we can't break."

She grabbed a paper napkin from a counter and with a bit of pencil she wrote: WE SWEAR TO SHARE THE ACTION BIKE NO MATTER WHAT HAPPENS FOREVER. We both signed. Maggie stuffed the napkin into her pocket, then we rushed over and bought one ticket with the extra money.

A big man in a red shirt and a baseball cap wrote our names on one half of the ticket and put it in a glass drum with a lot of others. He gave us the other half. Each half had the same number on it.

"I'll carry it," I said.

"No, I will," said Maggie. "It was my idea."

"Yeah, but who thought of writing it down? And who thought up the idea about Mr. Flynn's beard? I'm not a little baby, you know. You've got the napkin, I get the ticket." Maggie didn't have to run everything, I thought.

"Welllll," said Maggie.

"Awwwww, come on," I said. I guess I whined a little.

"Only if I get the bike first," Maggie agreed finally. It was a deal. We shook hands, then I got the ticket.

"Don't lose it," the man warned. "The draw is at 2:30."

"I won't," I said firmly.

But I did.

It might have happened anywhere: on the Space Race where we spun upside down way up in the air, or when the floor tipped in the Monster Mash, or when we were playing the games, or trying out a trampoline, or leaning over the pig pens, or petting the sheep, or climbing up on the fence of the horse ring. Maybe it was when we were tripping each other in the lineup for french fries or watching the man slice up vegetables with a special knife. Wherever it was, we found out as we were walking through the Pumpkin Palace, just starting to eat our french fries and planning how to share the bike. Maggie looked at her watch.

"It's almost time," she said. "Get out the ticket so we'll be ready."

I wiped my fingers on my pants and reached in my pocket. It was empty. I tried another; it was empty too. Then another and another and another, all empty. Then around again, faster and faster, poking and pulling my pockets inside out.

There was nothing there. "It's gone," I whispered.

"YOU LOST IT?" Maggie yelled. "Cyril, you DUMMY!" She was so mad she dropped the french fries. Neither of us cared. Above us the loudspeaker announced the bike draw in ten minutes.

"What do we do now?" I said. Tears pricked the corners of my eyes.

"We look for it," Maggie snapped, "quick."

But it was no use. We ran everywhere and checked everything and all we got was hot and sweaty. The ticket was gone for good.

Finally we stopped back at the entrance gate. "I guess we blew it," I sighed.

"Somebody did," said Maggie. She stared at me.

"YOUR ATTENTION PLEASE," blared the loudspeaker. "ON NOW IN THE PUMPKIN PALACE, DRAW FOR THE ACTION BIKE. THAT'S THE ACTION BIKE DRAW IN THE PUMPKIN PALACE. SHOW JUMPING IN THE HORSE RING IN FIFTEEN MINUTES."

"You just watch," I said, "our number will get called and we'll never know."

"Or somebody else will find our ticket and win," Maggie said, her mouth set tight.

I made a face and started to walk away. Then Maggie shouted, "Cyril, that's it! They won't just call our number, they'll call our names. Our names are on the other half of the ticket! Come on!'' The plan was on again.

A minute later we burst through the doors of the Pumpkin Palace. I could see the sign and the glass drum on the stage, but where was the bike?

We panted through a stream of people going the other way. By the time we got there the only person left was the man who had sold us the tickets.

"Where's the bike? When's the draw?'' I called.

The man shook his head. "I'm afraid you're too late, kids. The draw is over. The bike's already been won.''

"What?'' I said. "Didn't we win?''

"Not this time,'' the man said. "It was won by a girl named Maggie.''

"Maggie!'' screamed Maggie. "That's me.''

"And Cyril,'' I said, "Maggie and Cyril.''

The man smiled: "I remember now. You shared a ticket. Well, this was just a Maggie ticket, not Maggie and Cyril. I guess maybe there's lots of Maggies. Now go on and have some fun. There's lotsa things to do this afternoon.'' He started to take down the sign.

But we didn't care about other things any more. We walked back out of the Pumpkin Palace, past the dumb old pies and needlework and silly little-kid pictures. I didn't even care about the animals next door.

"It stinks around here," Maggie said. "Let's go back to the car."

"It's not three o'clock yet," I said. It didn't seem right to leave before we had to.

Maggie said, "Who cares," and I knew then she was right. It was time to go.

We didn't say much. I stubbed the toes of my runners in the dirt to kick up little puffs of dust. Maggie stomped on old bits of paper. It had been a pretty silly idea to think that we would win the bicycle, but it had just seemed so right that we would.

"Probably it wasn't a really good bike anyway," I said, not thinking that at all.

"Yeah," Maggie nodded, "they wouldn't give a good one away."

We went a little farther.

"Do you think anybody bought your house today?" I asked. Maggie just kept walking.

As we crossed the parking field we saw Maggie's mom and dad already at the car, putting something in the trunk.

"Did you buy something?" Maggie asked, coming up behind them. Maggie's dad started and nearly bumped his head on the trunk lid.

"Why are you two back so early?" said Maggie's mom.

"We just felt like it," Maggie said. "Did you buy something?"

Maggie's parents looked at each other. Maggie's dad said hesitatingly, "No, we won something. That is, *you* won something."

My stomach fluttered. Maggie's mom said, "We weren't going to tell you till we got home. There was a raffle at the fair, so we bought you each a ticket just for fun. Maggie's turned out to be lucky and she won—"

"A BICYCLE!" roared Maggie, and then we were climbing on the car to see. There it was in the trunk, our bike, the perfect bike, gleaming black and silver above its yellow wheels.

"Oh, wow," I gasped. I reached out to touch it, then remembered it wasn't my bike at all. *Our* ticket hadn't won. Slowly I drew my hand back.

"I hope you don't feel too bad, Cyril," said Maggie's dad. "It was just the luck of the draw."

"That's okay," I said, trying hard to sound as if it didn't matter at all.

Maggie was bouncing up and down. "I told him I was Maggie," she cheered, "I told him. I knew I was the one."

"Told who?" Maggie's mom asked, but Maggie was too excited to answer.

Maggie's dad got the bike out. "We'll have to adjust the seat," he said. Maggie rode it back and forth a couple of times anyway and tried a wheelie.

"It's fantastic," she called. "Thanks a lot."

"Maybe Cyril would like to try," said her mother.

"No, thank you," I muttered. It was all spoiled for me. How come Maggie always won?

Maggie's dad put the bike in the trunk again while Maggie gave him orders about watching out and not scratching it, then we all got in the car and started the trip home.

"Well, Maggie," said her mom, settling back as the car speeded up for the highway, "now all we need is a new house to go with your bike." She turned to us in the back seat. "And I know you'll let Cyril ride your new bike too, before we move. That ticket might just as easily have been his."

I stared out the window. Maggie said, "Uh-huh," but it didn't sound as if she meant it. Then she said all excited, "Just wait until the baby sees it. I can teach him to ride it when he's ready, can't I? I mean, I'll have to share with my brother."

"That will be a few years yet," said her mother, "and in the meantime you can share with Cyril. Besides, who says the Junior Partner is going to be a boy?"

"Awww," said Maggie, and started bugging her mom about babies. Babies and bicycles, I thought miserably. It didn't even matter to Maggie that we were partners any more. I wished I could shrink down into a tiny little speck that would blow out the window and fly away someplace else. Nobody wanted me around here, that was for sure.

After a while Maggie and her mom stopped talking. Then there was no sound but the rushing hum of the car. It made me feel dreary and tired.

After a while Maggie said to her parents, "Do you think somebody bought our house today?"

"Nobody can buy it until we say yes," her dad said, "but somebody might be interested. These things can happen fast."

"Oh," Maggie said.

I kept on looking out my window. Maggie looked out hers. Her parents started talking in low voices about houses and it came back to me that soon Maggie would be gone. Everything would be different. I leaned my head against the window and let the vibrations joggle through me. They made my teeth rattle. The old basketball-in-the-stomach feeling was coming back again.

From the corner of my eye I could see Maggie hunching forward, listening to her parents. She sat very still, frowning and biting at her lower lip. Her face was pale and her eyes were big and dark. Suddenly she looked at me; I looked quickly out the window. Then I heard her fumbling with something and she called out, "I forgot to tell you guys. Cyril and I made a deal about the bike a long time ago, just in case. See? We have to share it always.''

I whirled around. Maggie was handing the crumpled napkin with our deal written on it over the front seat. Her mother smoothed it out and read aloud: ''WE SWEAR TO SHARE THE ACTION BIKE NO MATTER WHAT HAPPENS FOREVER. But how did you know about the tickets?''

''It's very hard to explain,'' Maggie said. She looked my way for an instant.

''Very,'' I agreed. Right then I would have agreed with Maggie about anything.

''And how did you know you were going to win?'' her dad asked.

''Oh, that,'' Maggie yawned. ''We just knew.''

''Yeah.'' I yawned too.

''. . .SWEAR TO SHARE. . .NO MATTER WHAT. . .FOREVER.'' Maggie's mom was rereading the note. ''Well,'' she smiled, ''that'll make it hard for you to move too far away, won't it?''

''Gee,'' said Maggie, ''I never thought of that.''

She gave me a little kick in the ankle down behind the seat. I gave her foot a kick back and tried not to giggle. For now anyway, it looked as if we were sticking together.

Worms and Golf Balls

I was racing the new bike along a mountain road, skidding through turns to the very edge of the cliff, getting closer and closer to the bad guys, when the noon bell rang. I found myself riding my desk and chair instead.

"Okay," called Mr. Flynn, scratching where his beard was fuzziest. "People eating here, don't forget to take your coats now."

That was Maggie and me. My mom was being a substitute teacher more than ever and now Maggie's mom was busy looking for a house and getting ready to move, so we had to take our lunches to school. We got our stuff and went to the gym. As always, Maggie sat with the girls and I sat with the boys.

I was still dreaming about the bike. Today was my first day with it. Maggie had kept it nine whole days, but then she was grounded because

Elmer and Ugly Augie, the pet toads she wasn't supposed to have, escaped and scared the real estate lady when she was showing some people the bathroom in Maggie's house. The people left. They said that they were scared to look in the basement. Maggie got in trouble, the toads got put in the garden, and I got the bike.

Just as I started back on the mountain road a voice barked, "Shove over, shrimp." I was bumped along the bench and Ugly Augie sat down beside me. Not Ugly Augie the toad, but Ugly Augie Crumley the bully, the guy the toad was named after. He didn't usually pick on me too much any more because I hung around with Maggie and he was a little scared of her. She had tricked him a couple of times. Still, with guys like Ugly Augie you never can tell.

Bobby Devlin was with him, whispering and giggling about something in his lunch. That made me nervous. I watched while he and Ugly Augie gave Lester a piece of candy. "You have to eat it right now," Bobby said. As soon as Lester swallowed Bobby squealed, "EEWwwwwww, he ate it! Don't you know what it is? A chocolate-covered grasshopper! Oh, gross! Lester likes grasshoppers!"

Lester grabbed a napkin and tried to spit up, but it was too late; it was all gone. Lester looked as if he'd just seen that he'd sat in something awful. Bobby and Ugly Augie laughed like crazy, and at first I thought it was pretty funny too. I mean, who would be stupid enough to believe a candy was a chocolate-covered grasshopper?

I found out when they turned to me.

"Cyril's smarter," said Ugly Augie. "Hey, Cyril, want a chocolate-covered grasshopper?" He had another candy in his hand.

They weren't going to fool me and I wasn't going to look chicken either. "Oh sure," I said, and popped it in my mouth. "What is it, anyway?" I slurped.

"A grasshopper," Bobby said as I bit down. It *was* sort of crunchy. And it had a funny bitter taste. What if—no, it couldn't be—could it? All at once I didn't feel very well.

"We told you," Ugly Augie said, and they went away bent over with laughter.

Somehow I wasn't hungry any more.

"Did you see what those jerks did to me and Lester?" I asked Maggie when we went outside. "I wish they'd really get it."

Maggie shrugged. "Forget it, Cyril. Those guys are small fry. Besides, I've got my own problems: being grounded and finding out about the Junior Partner."

Forget it. That was easy for her to say. Maggie never got tricked, she just did the tricking. She never got picked on, she never looked dumb. It wasn't fair. I turned my head away from her and made the meanest face I could, to feel better. The grasshopper trick really bugged me but there was nothing I could do if Maggie didn't want to help out.

I tried to think of some way to persuade her but Maggie had already forgotten all about it. She was back on the Junior Partner again, bugging me about listening to my parents. I groaned.

"I'd listen if I were you, Cyril," Maggie warned, "because I've decided what the reward will be. If you find out that the Junior Partner is a boy for sure, you get the bike for an extra week!"

It felt like Christmas, my birthday and the last day of school all rolled into one. For about one second. Then I said suspiciously, "What if it's a girl?"

"Don't worry about that," Maggie said. "It won't be."

"How do you know?" I said.

"It has to be," said Maggie, "I just know." She just knew: that was Maggie for you.

"And what's so special about a baby brother anyway?" I said. "Who cares?"

"Are you kidding?" gasped Maggie. "Baby brothers are great! They're really neat to watch and have fun with and later when they get bigger you can play with them and show them stuff and—"

It was all so dumb it made me angry. "Is that ever stupid," I snorted. "All little babies do is cry and poop in their diapers. I have a baby cousin and that's all he ever does."

"Well, my brother will be smarter than that," sniffed Maggie. "Besides, I didn't mean right now, I meant when he gets older. I can show him how to ride the bike and take him up in the treehouse and—"

"But that's all our stuff," I yelled.

"You'll just have to share," said Maggie. I decided I'd better do my riding now.

After school I took the bike and rode down the block from Greenapple Street to Maple Avenue, past this big old house that was for sale. Lately I was noticing houses for sale everywhere. The sign on this one made the perfect halfway marker for the race I was pretending to have with Bobby and Ugly Augie. Every time I got to my place I won the race and everybody cheered. The losers always begged for another race, so I'd beat them again no matter what they tried.

I won about fourteen races in a row and went in feeling good. Then my dad called from the kitchen, "It's worms and golf balls for dinner," and my stomach hit my ankles. It was like lunch all over again.

My dad laughed. "I mean spaghetti and meat

balls. That's what we called them when I was a kid."

I ate carefully anyway. And when I heard it was school lunch again tomorrow I stopped eating completely. That strange, crunchy taste came back into my mouth. I brushed my teeth extra hard that night.

The next day they were up to the same stupid tricks, but what happened this time changed everything. Bobby and Ugly Augie started by daring Monica to eat a peanut butter sandwich. When she bit in all this red stuff oozed out. Monica started to cry and Maggie, who was right beside her, said, "Buzz off, Bobby. It's just peanut butter and ketchup. If you're so smart, eat it yourself."

It was then that Bobby and Ugly Augie made history.

Bobby said, "Why not? We've got two." He grabbed the next sandwich and ate some. Then he gave it to Augie and he did the same. "Mmmmm," Bobby said, "now you have one. Or are you chicken?"

It got very quiet. Nobody ever, ever tried to pick on Maggie. I held my breath and watched. Maggie hated all kinds of regular food and loved some stuff that was extra disgusting. She did like ketchup, but could she eat this?

Maggie's hand shot out. She grabbed Monica's sandwich, bit and swallowed as fast as she could, almost without chewing.

"SHE ATE IT! SHE ATE IT!" Bobby and Ugly Augie went crazy. "Oh, what a dummy! Fooled you! Ever sick! Yuck, yuck, yuck!" They grabbed their stomachs as if they were going to throw up.

Maggie said, "So what? You ate it too." She looked suspicious.

Bobby looked as if he was going to explode with laughter. Augie said, "Oh yeah?" and slowly lifted their sandwich. There was no ketchup. The impossible had just happened: Maggie had been fooled.

For a second everyone was stunned. Then one kid giggled. And another, then more joined in and the giggles turned to laughs and the laughs to shouts. Maggie's face went red and her cheek began to twitch. I got ready for her to cream them right then and there, but suddenly she changed. She sighed instead. She rolled her eyes. She tapped her foot. She waited. Finally, in a voice that sounded as if she didn't want to bother, she said, "I'm going to have to do something about this." She sighed again, louder this time.

Bobby and Augie pretended to beg for mercy and everybody laughed again. Maggie just yawned, sat down and started to eat.

I sat there with my mouth full of tuna fish. Part

of me was horrified, part of me was glad it hadn't happened to me, and a tiny little part was glad that Maggie had been fooled, just once. But what would she do now? She didn't say a word until we lined up to go out. Then she whispered, "Cyril, this means war." I didn't know whether to cheer or find a place to hide.

By recess it was raining and we had to stay in. A bunch of us sat around talking about how Bobby and Ugly Augie were bugging everybody. When I told how my dad scared me by saying we were having worms and golf balls for dinner, Maggie jumped up and took off. When she came back she tried to hide something under her sweater, but I saw. She had a library book about food.

It was still raining when we walked home from school, coming down way too hard for me to ride the bike. Maggie was smiling though, as if the sun were shining at the start of summer holidays.

"I've got plans, Cyril," she announced. "One takes care of being grounded and one takes care of the lunch problem."

"What are you going to do?"

"Not me, Cyril. *We*. We're partners, right?"

"Yeah, but—"

"Right," said Maggie, "so you have to help, especially since I'm grounded. We'll really fix those bozos."

I knew what that meant. I'd do all the silly stuff

and get in trouble and Maggie would end up with everyone telling her how smart she was. The last thing I wanted was to get stuck in one of Maggie's plans, especially one to get Augie Crumley. He liked pounding people just my size.

I tried to get out of it. "Oh, yeah?" I said. "Well, if we're partners, how come you didn't start a plan when they picked on me?"

"I was busy, Cyril," Maggie said. "I'm still working on being grounded, remember? And besides, this is different. I mean, if they're going to pick on everybody we have to do something, right?"

"I guess," I said, unconvinced. Then I had a great idea. If I was going to risk a pounding from Augie I was going to get paid for it. And I knew what I wanted. I said, "But I'm only helping if I get the bike for an extra week."

"What!" shrieked Maggie. "No way, Cyril, you sneak!" She yelled and screamed, but I knew she was stuck. This time it was Maggie who had a problem and she needed me to help.

I was already making my plans for the extra week when Maggie said, "But I'm not doing this for me, you know, Cyril. It's for you. I'm going to be moving soon and Ugly Augie won't be picking on *me* after that. He'll have to pick on whoever's left behind. Whoever he thinks is shrimpy and scared, you know?"

I froze. I had never thought about what would happen when Maggie moved: Ugly Augie would be king of the schoolyard and it would be open season for picking on Cyril. I remembered what it was like to get picked on all the time, before Maggie helped me out the first time. Suddenly, somehow, I was in big trouble.

"Yup," said Maggie as if she'd read my mind, "you'll be in big trouble. Unless I make you look like a big tough hero now, the kind nobody would ever dare to pick on."

"How?" I gasped.

"Just do everything I say," said Maggie, "and give *me* the bike for an extra week." I moaned and groaned but she had me. We shook hands and I got ready to be a hero. "First," said Maggie, "you gather up some worms."

So I squished around the back yard putting worms in a plastic dish and getting rain down my neck while Maggie stayed dry in the garage. When I was done I took in the worms. Maggie had a cardboard box, a bag labelled PEAT MOSS and the food book sitting on her work table. She dumped some of the peat moss in the box and spread it around. It was like dark, crumbly dirt. Then she put in the worms. They lay there in a lump for a minute, then they began to untangle themselves and ooze off under the moss.

"There," said Maggie, "now we have to wait

twenty-four hours for the worms to be ready."

I had a terrifying thought. "You're not going to make them eat worms, are you? I mean, not really?"

Maggie groaned. "Cyyyyrullllll. Don't forget, there's two plans. Now, today's Wednesday. Thursday we wait. Friday we take care of Augie and Bobby. Saturday my dad is going fishing."

"Oh, I get it. If you do something nice for your dad maybe you won't be grounded so long, so you gathered up worms for fishing."

"That's right," said Maggie. "Almost."

Almost? I figured I had it but Maggie didn't want to say so. "But what about our plan?"

"We just started it," Maggie said. "The plans are tied together. The next part you have to do is to keep the worms in your garage. After what happened with the toads I'd really get it for hiding worms."

I went home confused. That night my mom said she wasn't working tomorrow so I could come home for lunch. Maggie was invited too.

"Good," I said. No chocolate-covered grasshoppers tomorrow, anyway.

"It's hard for you when I work, isn't it?" said my mom. "I understand." She didn't exactly, but I let her hug me anyway.

The next night, Thursday, Maggie phoned me after supper. "This is it, Cyril," she hissed.

"Bring the worms to my back door, I'll be waiting."

I asked if I could go to Maggie's for a while, then I put on my jacket, went out to the garage and peeked in. The garage was spooky at night. Strange shapes lurked in the dark. I took a deep breath, dashed in and was out with the worms in one second flat. I didn't look back, either.

Maggie's back door swung open as soon as I got there. Maggie silently handed me the plastic dish and a note and slipped back inside. The note read: Put WORMS in dish. Put PEAT MOSS in garden. Put BOX at garbage tin. Knock on door. P.S. Get rid of NOTE.

I did it all and tore up the note. I was going to eat it, like on TV, but the first bit tasted awful, almost as bad as the grasshopper. I stuffed the rest in my pocket instead and knocked on the door.

Maggie answered. "It's Cyril with my stuff for school," she called into the house. To me she whispered, "Don't say 'worms'."

We went up into the kitchen. As I took off my jacket I looked around and tried to understand. On the stove was a pot of steaming water and a frying pan. On the counter sat a bottle of cooking oil, vinegar, spice jars, little piles of chopped onion and red pepper, a bag of noodles, butter, tongs, a mixing bowl, plastic dishes, oven mitts, a

54

knife, a loaf of bread, sandwich wrap, a recipe book and the food book from school. Maggie hid the dish of worms behind the noodles and put a lid over part of it.

Just then Maggie's mom came in to say hi. She warned Maggie to be careful and call if she wanted any help. "The Junior Partner and I will be watching the news," she said and went into the den.

"Is your mom helping?" I asked.

"She gave me a recipe," Maggie said. "Now, let's get busy."

She put me to work buttering bread, then turned up the heat on the stove. When the water boiled Maggie dumped in a bunch of noodles and set the timer.

"Which plan is this?" I asked.

"Both," said Maggie, and made me wash off the worms in the sink, one at a time.

"C'mon, what are we making?" I asked.

"Something for fishing, something for tomorrow." Maggie stirred the noodles.

I tried again. "But what things?"

"Okay," Maggie said, talking low, "I'll give you a hint. You can do lots of things with noodles, you know? You can boil them to make them soft and then make noodle salad when they're cold, or you can boil them and then fry them up with butter. They turn all goldy brown and squiggly and crispy." Maggie's eyes got big. "Yup," she said, "all goldy brown. And squiggly. Ugly looking. They taste different too. Get it?" She turned to the stove. "Of course, you can do that with other stuff too."

The timer buzzed. Maggie picked up the tongs.

"Coming," called Maggie's mom from the den.

"Five minutes," Maggie yelled back. Now she was in a big rush. "I'll finish this, Cyril. Your part comes tomorrow. Get ready to be a hero." She hustled me to the door.

As I went out I whispered, "I think I get it."

"Good," said Maggie and shut the door fast.

In fact, I was sure I got it. I went home and asked my mom if she was working tomorrow. "I'm afraid so, dear," she said. I said, "So I have to take my lunch, right? Great!" She looked pretty surprised as I went upstairs.

By next morning I was absolutely positive. Maggie was definitely a genius. And since I figured it out all by myself, I was no dummy either.

"I get it," I giggled proudly to Maggie as we walked to school, but Maggie was all business. "Listen, Cyril," she said, "at lunch if I give you something to eat, just eat. Don't ask questions till after and you'll be a big hero. Okay?"

"Sure, sure," I insisted. "Don't worry. *I get it.*"

Boy, did I ever.

By lunch I was so excited I could barely sit. For once, I thought, I knew what was going to happen and it was going to be great. It sure felt good to be in on the whole trick for a change. I watched in the gym as Bobby and Ugly Augie teased George that he was scared to eat some shriveled-up pepperoni sticks. Bobby said they were fingers off a dead body. Then I saw Maggie grab some stuff and stroll over behind them. I ran to catch up, then slowed down and tried to walk cool instead, like a hero.

We watched for a second, then Maggie nudged me. As George opened his mouth to bite I shouted, "Wait." Everything stopped. Bobby and Augie turned.

"Whadda *you* want?" Augie sneered. He sure wasn't scared of Maggie now. But I wasn't scared of him either. This time I *knew*.

"They want ketchup and grasshoppers," said Bobby. They snickered behind their hands.

"We don't want anything," said Maggie. "We've got something for you." She put the stuff down on the desk. There was a plastic dish with a lid on, a package of sandwiches and the food book.

"Since you guys always have stuff to share with us," Maggie said, "we brought something to share with you. Right, Cyril?"

"Right," I said. I crossed my arms and puffed out my chest hero-style.

"So," Maggie said, "I made some worm sandwiches for all of us." She opened the package while I concentrated on looking tough. Inside were two sandwiches cut in half, the curvy crust on one half and the straight crust on the other. Four sandwich halves. I knew it, I thought.

Bobby and Augie looked at the sandwiches. For a second they seemed a tiny bit scared. Then Bobby said, "Yeah, *sure*."

"They are," said Maggie. "See?" She opened one of the halves. On the buttered bread was a jumble of, well, things. Crispy, goldy brown, squiggly things. I knew it, I thought, I knew it, I knew it. Fried noodle sandwiches. It was hard not to laugh. Kids crowded around and little gasps went up when they saw what was in the sandwiches. Bobby and Ugly Augie were surrounded now and they looked worried. I bit my cheeks hard, trying not to laugh.

"This isn't pretend stuff," Maggie said. "You have to be tough to eat these." Maggie gave me a half with a straight crust. I took a big bite and tried to chew. The fried noodles didn't have much taste but they felt nice in my mouth. "They're better with ketchup," I growled and ripped off another bite. The crowd oohed and aahed. I pretended not to notice.

"Looks like Cyril's tough enough," Maggie said. "Let's see if you two are. I'll even split each sandwich so there's no tricks like before." She gave Augie the curvy half of my sandwich. Bobby got a curvy half and Maggie kept the other straight one. I remembered Maggie hated curvy crusts. Bobby and Augie held the sandwiches as if they might explode.

"What's the matter?" Maggie asked. "Chicken?"

"It's just a trick," Augie snarled. "That wimp wouldn't eat worms. Come on." He tore into the sandwich. Bobby watched, then bit in slowly. A couple of girls giggled and the boys made sick noises behind them.

Augie finished first. "Ha ha ha, very funny," he said. He wasn't laughing. In fact, he looked ready to do some pounding. "Now, what was it really?" The giggling stopped.

"It was worms," said Maggie. "Ask Cyril, he collected them."

I nodded. What now? I thought. It looked as if they weren't going to be fooled. For the first time that day I was scared. What if this didn't work? Ugly Augie would pound me for sure.

Maggie said, "I'll show you. Worms are good for you and everything. It says so right here." She put down her sandwich half and opened the food book. "What you do is get the worms and put them in peat moss for twenty-four hours. That cleans them out. We did that, right, Cyril?" I nodded again. Now I was getting mixed up as well as scared. Maggie went on. "Then you rinse them off—Cyril did that and put them in boiling water for three minutes."

Something lurched in my stomach. I said, "Wait a—", but Maggie didn't stop. "Then you fry them with butter until they're goldy brown and crispy and squiggly. Cyril had to leave early so I did those bits and made sandwiches, right, Cyril?"

A swampy feeling started to spread from my middle. It couldn't be true. 'No," I blurted. "The worms were for your dad. For fishing!"

Maggie looked puzzled. "My dad doesn't fish with worms," she said calmly. "He uses fishing lures." The feeling climbed into my throat. I didn't care if I wrecked the plan or not, anything was better than finding out I'd just eaten worms.

"But you were making noodles," I yelled. "Worms for fishing, noodles for sandwiches!"

"Oh, no," said Maggie. "You must have got confused. *Noodles* for fishing, *worms* for sandwiches."

"WHAT?"

"I made noodles for noodle salad," Maggie said. "My dad loves it for lunch when he goes fishing. Me too. I've got some for lunch today, see?" She opened the plastic dish. Inside was a mess of soggy noodles with red pepper and onion bits in oil and vinegar dressing. "I told you," said Maggie, "worms for sandwiches."

I shrieked. Everybody else in the room squealed and gagged, except Bobby and Ugly Augie. They raced for the washroom, and I was right behind them, until Maggie grabbed my shirt-tail.

"Remember what I promised," she hissed.

My stomach rolled like the ocean. "But you tricked me," I moaned. "Let me go. I think I'm going to be sick."

"Act like a hero, Cyril. Watch me," Maggie snapped. She grabbed her sandwich half and bit the middle. "That's that," she said as loud as she could with her mouth full. "Those dimwits aren't bothering us again." She took another bite and leaned in close. "Besides, *you* didn't eat worms. I'm not eating them now."

I stared.

"I fried the worms but I fried a few noodles too. They got the worms and we got noodles. I had to trick you or they wouldn't have believed me. Just don't tell anybody."

My stomach began to feel better. Then it heaved again. "But Augie and I ate from the same sandwich."

Maggie snickered. "I cut the sandwiches first

and put different stuff in each half. That way it looked like we were sharing." She took another bite.

A wave of relief rolled over me. I sat down on a bench so my legs wouldn't tremble so much. I was panting as if I'd just run around the schoolyard.

Maggie sat down beside me and whispered proudly, "All I had to do was remember which half had which. It was easy." She waved her sandwich crust. Maggie always saved the crust for last. "See, I thought I'd put the worms in the curvy halfs because I hate curvy crusts, so I started to, but then I thought what if they know I hate them, so I put the worms in the straight-crust halfs to be extra careful, and just this once I ate a curvy crust for a good cause, even if it is yucky." She stopped. "Hey, what's the matter with you?"

Slowly I looked up at Maggie, then back down. I nodded my head very carefully, and Maggie's gaze travelled down to the crust in her hand.

It was straight.

For a second we just looked at each other. Then we headed for the washrooms. Fast—but like heroes.

Substitute Mother

The fried worms trick did make us heroes, sort of. We got in trouble, but Bobby and Augie quit teasing everybody, and after a while I was even glad Maggie had mixed up the sandwiches: now I knew I really was tough enough to eat worms.

Things quieted down on Greenapple Street. People came and went at Maggie's place and her mom and dad looked all over for a new house, but nothing changed. Sometimes it was easy to forget they had to move. Maggie and I went to school and swapped the bike back and forth. She seemed to get it more than me somehow. Maggie's mom got bigger with the Junior Partner, but we were becoming used to that. Even Mr. Flynn's beard began to look right.

The autumn rains came. Leaves turned orange and yellow before they fell and the cold snuck in. One clear morning we woke up to find the ground white with frost. I started hoping for snow. Best of all, my mom didn't work so much as a substitute teacher. Once she was home almost a whole week and things were just like they used to be. I wanted them to stay that way forever.

We were still eating Hallowe'en candy when the first kids got the flu. It was a special bad flu, all the way from Hong Kong, and pretty soon it seemed like everybody was getting it. At the start I wanted to get sick and stay home too, but school felt different with everybody away, like a private club almost, so I changed my mind. Besides with all the flu going around my mom was working every day, plus my dad had to go away to a big meeting so I couldn't get sick: there was no one to look after me. But then I thought if I did get sick maybe my mom would have to quit substitute teaching and stay home for good to look after me. I pretended to be sick, just to see. My mom sent me to school anyway, which made me pretty mad. I mean, I could have been sick and then what would have happened? Something awful, that's what.

It didn't though. I kept right on going to school and so did Maggie and not much of anything happened, until one day when Mr. Flynn said that even though there were people away our true/false quiz on Japan was going to be tomorrow. Suddenly I wanted to be sick for sure.

That night Maggie came over to study with me while her parents went to look at a house. My mom helped us by asking us questions about Japan. Maggie did great, as always. I did terrible, but my mom didn't seem to notice. She yawned a lot.

"How come you're so tired?" I asked, partly so she wouldn't ask me another Japan question.

My mom smiled. "Oh, it's just a busy time, that's all, and Daddy's been at the conference all week and can't help around here like he usually does. So I guess I'm a little bit pooped." She puffed out her cheeks in a sigh. "Anyway, it doesn't matter. Tomorrow's Friday and your dad will be home on the weekend."

"You should quit," I said hopefully.

"It's not as bad as all that. Besides, I can't quit if I want to be a full-time teacher again."

A *what*? Nobody had told me about this. Before I could say anything the phone rang. Maggie's parents were home and she was off.

The phone was ringing again when I woke up the next morning. "Guess where I'm working to-day?" my mom said at breakfast. "Your school. You'll still have to take your lunch though. I won't have time to come home."

The more I thought about it the better it seemed. With my mom working at my school I'd be special for sure. I imagined walking up to her in the hall and talking about school stuff just like teachers did with each other, while everyone watched. I got all excited until my mom handed me my lunch and said, "Good luck on the test."

A Friday never seems like a Friday when you have a test. It's like a mountain standing in the way of Saturday. "Maybe so many people will be away we won't have it," I said to Maggie as we walked to school. I told her about my mom, too.

But Maggie didn't want to talk about that stuff. Instead she went back to the same old thing: "Did your mom talk to mine on the phone after I left last night? Late, I mean."

"I dunno," I said, "I don't think so."

"You don't think so?" snorted Maggie. "Are you spying or what? How am I going to find out for sure that the Junior Partner is a boy if you don't do your job?"

"Hey," I said, "I had to go to bed, you know."

"Don't you sneak around?" Maggie sounded amazed. "After bed is the best time. Parents always talk when they think you're asleep."

"Well, my mom didn't talk to your mom," I said, "I'm pretty sure." I wasn't really, but I was tired of Maggie picking at me. It really bugged me sometimes.

Maggie said nervously, "Hmmm. Well, just remember, Cyril. Help me find out I'm getting a brother and you get the bike for a whole extra week. . .and first ride when we share."

"Wow!" I roared. Maggie must really be getting desperate. "Even when the Junior Partner rides?"

"He'll have to go after," said Maggie. "After all, it's *our* bike. Besides, he won't be ready for a couple of years."

Now Friday seemed a lot more like Friday, even with a test. I was feeling pretty happy as I walked into Room 7—until things went haywire.

My mother was sitting at Mr. Flynn's desk. I rushed to the front of the room. "Where's Mr. Flynn?" I whispered. Something was very wrong.

"He has the flu," my mom said. "I didn't find out till I got here. So surprise, surprise, I'm your substitute teacher."

"But you can't be," I said.

"Of course I can be," she said. "Why not?"

"But you're my mom! Isn't there a rule or something?"

"No, there isn't. I'm your mom but I'm also a teacher, and that's what I'm being right now. I'll explain to the class and it will be fine. Remember, I know some of them already. And don't worry, Cyril, I've done this before, you know."

"Ohhhhhh," I moaned and looked around quickly. Already kids were looking at us and whispering. I gulped. Terrible thoughts crowded into my mind about having your mom teach your class. She'd know everything you did; you'd have to be good all the time and then you'd get called a goody-goody. If she was too strict, everybody would blame you. If she was silly, everybody would laugh at you. And our class was rotten for substitute teachers. What if Bobby started making gross noises and gabby Monica wanted to talk forever and Lester and George started a spitball fight? My toes curled up as I pictured it.

Then came the worst thought of all: what if my mom forgot and called me something she called me at home, like "pumpkin"? If my mother called me pumpkin in class I'd shrivel up and die.

"Can't you trade?" I pleaded. My mom said no. I was sunk. All I could do was lean close and mutter, "Just don't call me pumpkin."

My mom smiled. "I won't," she said, and she didn't. In fact, she never called me anything.

At first I didn't mind. After the announcements my mom told the class who she was and explained that Mr. Flynn was sick. I tried to shrink, but everybody else just looked curious. My mom called everybody she knew by name. They all sat up straighter, as if they were special. Hmmpf, I thought. Then Monica asked if we were having the test.

"Yes," my mom said, "right after lunch." Everybody groaned. Then she told us what else Mr. Flynn had left for us and we started working.

My mom made some jokes, and kids laughed, but you could tell she meant business. When Bobby stuck his hand in his armpit and made gross noises she asked him nicely if he'd like to stay in at recess and practise. And when Monica kept yacking and yacking she gave her a long tricky part to read out loud. She was pretty quiet after that. For Monica, anyway.

I started to feel that things might turn out okay. Maybe Mr. Flynn would be sick for a week, I thought hopefully. Because if everybody was going to like my mom I was going to become a Very Important Person. Special things to do, lots of homework help, kids being nice to me: I saw it all.

But my mom didn't seem to see me. It was as if she forgot I was there. She never noticed my hand, I never got to go to the board, I got the dullest bit to read out loud. Other kids got to clap the chalk brushes, hold the door, show everybody their work, be monitor at the drinking fountain. And it wasn't as if I was goofing around either. She noticed the ones who were. For a while I did my best to goof around, too. It wasn't until I was trying to balance an eraser on the end of my nose instead of doing Silent Reading that my mom paid any attention to me. Without looking up, she said, "Cyril, nose in your book, not eraser on your nose, please," and went right on making notes.

And that was that. Everybody liked my mom and I was still just dumb old Cyril. I couldn't even go home at lunch and complain. I guessed I knew now why my mom wanted to work: she could spend the day with neater kids and not have to bother with me. I wanted to do something really smart so everybody would notice. I dreamed up a lot of things, then I remembered the test; I could do great on the test! Except I'd done rotten at studying. I went back to feeling crummy again.

Lunchtime came. I went up to the front so the others would see me with my mom, but she was talking with George and Lester. They knew her from coming to my house. I waited and waited. Just as I was going to butt in, the word *Japan* jumped out at my eye. I looked again and a secret, scary arrow of excitement ran through me. Peeking out from a folder on the teacher's desk was the quiz on Japan, *with the answers marked in*!

I looked away fast, but my mom was still talking. Now I could do better than great on the test: I could get perfect. I moved closer to the desk. Nobody was paying attention. Then a voice inside said, *If you look you'll be a cheater*. I stopped. I tried to study, I thought, it was just that—that my mom was tired. But the feeling didn't go away. I thought, it's not as if I'm hurting anybody. It's not really cheating if you don't get caught. *Yes, it is*, said the voice. I wriggled around and answered that I wasn't doing it for the mark, but just because everything was so unfair today that I needed some help. It was just lucky for me, that's all. She didn't leave the test out for everyone to see, I just accidentally saw it. Anyway, I was doing it for my mom, not me. So she'd be proud. *Cheater*, said the voice. I ignored it and turned to the desk.

As I looked back at the paper I felt hot all over. I was scared stiff somebody would see me before I was done, but nobody did. I learned all the answers and cleared out fast. I'd get noticed soon enough.

I had lunch by myself, repeating the answers over and over. I didn't eat much. I wanted to feel happy, but I didn't. The gym felt hot and stuffy. I went outside as soon as I could. After the bell I was first in my seat. Everybody took out pencils and waited. Voices buzzed around me in the warm room. My mind felt fuzzy and for a second I was scared I might forget the answers. My stomach squirmed. I *had* to get perfect.

The quiz papers got passed out face down. "Quiet, please," said my mom. "No talking until the papers are collected. You have fifteen minutes, starting now."

There was a rustle of paper as we began. I wrote all the answers as fast as I could and slapped down my pencil. A couple of kids looked up. Dummy, I thought. Finishing too fast looked suspicious. I went back and carefully darkened in each answer. It was still too soon to finish. I used up some more time reading the questions and found I even knew some of the answers. I was glad about that. It wasn't really cheating if I could have answered anyway. *Yes, it is*, said the voice.

I picked up my pencil again to darken in my name. The room was getting warmer and warmer and the lights hummed in my head. Somebody's wet socks were smelling. The air felt like a big cotton ball pressing me down. It made me so tired I didn't even care much about the test any more.

"Five minutes," said my mom. I kept my head down and closed my eyes. Something heavy was sitting just above my stomach. It got even hotter. I knew I'd felt like this before, but I couldn't remember what it meant. My mouth began to water. The cotton ball was too stuffy to breathe; I needed some air. The weight above my stomach shifted. Then I knew what it all meant and I put up my hand, fast, but it was too late. I was sick all over my perfect test paper. Twice.

The next thing I knew Maggie was leading me down the hall to the office, keeping one step ahead all the way. The secretary cleaned me up a little, then took me to a room across the hall where there was a couch to lie on.

"You just hang on, Cyril," she said. "We'll get you fixed up. It looks like the Hong Kong flu has caught you."

I lay there feeling rotten. Everything was all wrong: my mom was my teacher, I was a cheater, and the only time anybody noticed me was when I threw up. And now I remembered there was no one to look after me even if I *was* sick. I groaned. Maybe I'd have to go to the hospital all by myself. In an ambulance with a siren. I felt lonely and scared. Not even the thought of the ambulance ride cheered me up.

There was a clatter of voices and footsteps in the hall, then my mom came in with our coats. "Come on, pumpk— Cyril," she said. "It's time to get you home."

I didn't understand. "But you can't," I said, "you're the teacher."

"I'm also your mother," said my mom, "and right now that's what's important."

"But what about the class? Are you fired?"

My mom smiled. "No, no, the principal says she'll look after the class this afternoon. Now come on."

At home I sank into the cool sheets of my bed. My room felt like the best place in the world. My mom took my temperature, then told me to go to sleep. I wanted to ask a question first though:

"What will happen to my test?"

"Well," said my mom, "Mr. Flynn will probably make up another one for people who missed it. You can take that."

"Another quiz!" I said. "But—"

"Let's call it another chance," said my mom. "Remember, I helped you study and I think you might have needed more than one."

"Awwwww," I moaned.

"I'll help you study if there is another test," said my mom.

That reminded me of something else. "But what if you're too tired if you're a full-time teacher?" I asked.

My mom sat down on the bed. "One thing at a time, Cyril. Teaching jobs are hard to get and even if I was lucky and got one, it wouldn't be until next year. We'll see how it goes. But your dad and I will always do our best to have lots of time for you."

"But then why don't you want to stay home always?" I asked.

"Because when I earn some money it's easier for us to make ends meet. And, because I think you're a big enough guy now that you don't need your mom around every second. And most of all because I like being a teacher and working with boys and girls. I learn things doing it." My mom smiled.

74

I thought it over. I didn't know about the money stuff. I guessed she was right about me being big enough; I was no baby. But teachers learning things? That was weird.

After a second my mom asked, "Do you think I did okay today?"

I was scared about what to say. I tried some little things first: "Well. . .you could write on the board bigger?"

"Uh-huh," said my mom.

"And Mr. Flynn always picks best worker to hold the door, not the quietest."

"Good idea," she nodded. She didn't sound mad. I tried a hint about something bigger. "You should split up the reading out loud so everybody gets a good part."

"Mmmm," my mom said, "that can be hard to do, but yes."

I tried again, very softly: "Everybody should get a chance to do stuff."

"That's for sure," she said. "Why, was someone left out?"

This was it. I shrank down beneath the covers and whispered, "You didn't call on *me* much."

"What?" She looked really surprised. "Yes I—I thought I—well. . .hmmm. Well, maybe you're right. And do you know why? I saw your hand go up and I knew you were trying but I thought if I called on you a lot the others would say you were my favourite and pick on you. Then you were sick, so I never had a chance to tell you how well you did today.''

"Oh.'' I had never thought of getting picked on for being the favourite. "Did I really do good?'' I asked. My mom nodded and suddenly I was glad I got sick on my test. I mean, if I had to be sick I was glad it was there, I guess. I asked one more question. "Will you ever have another baby? Like Maggie's mom?''

"No, Cyril,'' said my mom, "I don't think so. You're enough for us. Now go to sleep.''

I closed my eyes and she gave me a kiss on the forehead. Mothers are like that: they always wait till you're not looking.

When I woke up my mom was talking on the phone, telling someone I was sick. I listened for more about me, but instead she said: "How's the real estate dealing coming along? Oh really. . . . Tonight, uh-huh, well good luck. . . .''

Who was she talking to, I wondered.

Then she said, "Anyway, you were saying last night about the tests you had back in September? Uh-huh, uh-huh. . . . DID you? Oh, really. . . . And they told you what the baby's going to be?'' Something about those words was important, but I couldn't remember what. Then all of a sudden my mom said, "Oh my goodness, you're *kidding*. That's incredible! Were you surprised? What does

John think? . . .Well, of course. . . ." She laughed. "What does Maggie think?"

I sat straight up. It was Maggie's mom on the phone. They were talking about the Junior Partner. I held my breath and listened as hard as I could. My mom laughed again. "I'll bet she wasn't too pleased about that. Did she hatch a plot to find out? . . .Uh-huh. . . . I don't know how you kept it secret *this* long. . . . Right, keep her busy. . . . No harm done. . . . Well, I won't tell Cyril."

She wouldn't, huh? I'd see about that. Except I couldn't hold my breath much longer. They talked some more and my mom said, "Which does she want, boy or girl? Mmm, uh-huh. . . ." I thought I was going to explode. Then my mom said, "Well, she got more than she bargained for, didn't she? She's going to have both with twins."

I was so surprised I nearly fell out of bed. Twins! Junior Partners! I whooshed out a long breath and flopped back into my pillow. For the first time in a long while everything felt terrific, even if I was sick. I even knew something big before Maggie.

I scrunched down under the covers with my new secret and went back to sleep, already dreaming about a new week with the bike and wondering what Maggie would say about twins.

Saturday morning I was still sick. From the front window Greenapple Street looked dull and soggy and the street lights still glowed in the grey sky. There were puddles along the side of the road. I looked hard, but I didn't see Maggie. I saw something else though, something that made me forget all about babies and bicycles. Plastered across the For Sale sign on Maggie's front lawn was a sticker that read Sold.

The More Things Change . . .

It was the last day of November, moving day. I was bouncing my feet to keep warm as I sat on my front steps, watching the big truck get loaded up at Maggie's. I stuffed my hands deep into my coat pockets and sighed. Maggie wasn't around anywhere that I could see. I didn't know if I was angry or sad; Maggie had been acting so strange lately.

After I'd seen the Sold sticker that Saturday three weeks ago I had to wait till the next Wednesday to see Maggie. She'd got the flu after I did. I tried to think of a plan for us, but I was no good at it. Maggie was the Greenapple Street Genius, not me. She'd think of something, I told myself, and tried to forget. But every time I came up Greenapple Street those big orange letters stared back at me: Sold. Something told me no plan could change that.

When Maggie did come back to school, she wasn't much help. She was just as glum as I was. She told us all that her family had to find a place to move to by the end of November. After school we walked up Greenapple Street, shuffling through the piles of leaves and having dumb ideas that always began "What if. . ." or "Maybe. . .", but it was no use, we had to give up.

"What do you want to do now?" I asked.

"Let's take turns on the bike," Maggie answered.

We timed ourselves riding around the block down to Maple Avenue and back up. Racing the bike made me feel better. Whipping down Greenapple Street with the wind at my back made the end of November seem a long way away. But then I'd turn down and over onto Maple Avenue, pedalling standing up with the wind in my face and go by the big house there that still had a For Sale sign and I'd remember and wish Maggie's house was still for sale. I'd turn up and around again and sail down Greenapple Street with the wind until I flew past those letters again: Sold.

"They should have bought the house on Maple Avenue instead of your place," I said to Maggie. She just nodded and sighed.

After dinner Maggie came over while her parents went to look at more houses with the real estate lady. We did our homework, and when it was time for her to go my dad asked her if she was looking forward to the Junior Partner's arrival.

"What are you hoping for," asked my dad, "a brother or a sister?"

I hadn't thought about the Junior Partner for a long time, and it wasn't until Maggie said, "A brother," that I remembered my secret: the baby was babies. The Junior Partners were twins.

"Hey!" I blurted out. "I—"

Everybody turned to me. "I. . .forget," I said. I couldn't tell Maggie in front of my mom and dad. Maggie was already out the door anyway. Tomorrow I'd tell her for sure, I promised myself, but by the time I finished watching TV, I had already forgotten all about it.

That was how things went for the next while. After school we'd ride the bike and after dinner Maggie would come over while her parents looked at houses. Then I'd wait till the next morning to hear from Maggie that they hadn't found anything. Time was running out, and just as I was starting to hope that maybe they'd never find a house, everything changed—Maggie most of all.

After school one day she came out of her place looking worried. "I have to go with my parents tonight," she said.

"To see a house?" I said. She nodded. "Where?"

"I don't know," said Maggie, "but it looks like they mean business."

After that not even bike riding was fun. Even when I was faster neither of us much cared. Every time I went along Maple Avenue and saw that big empty house it just seemed more unfair.

The next morning though, Maggie was all smiles, so I knew what had happened. "The house stunk, right?" I said.

"No," said Maggie, "the house was FAN-tastic! I really want to move there for sure."

For a second I couldn't feel anything at all. I said, "You *want* to move?"

"For sure," said Maggie. "I'm not supposed to say yet, but wait till I tell you—"

But I didn't want to hear. All at once I was angrier than I had ever been in my whole life. "Who cares," I said, then ran by myself all the way to school.

The rest of that day I felt as if I had chewed a lemon. Maggie tried to talk to me a couple of times but I just turned away. Finally she said, "Okay, Cyril, be that way. See if I care." She smiled her I've-got-a-secret smile and strolled away. I stuck out my tongue. She could move to Siberia for all I cared.

After school I went home and didn't even come

out when I saw Maggie on our bike. What made it worse was that she looked so happy. She'd probably wanted to move all along, I told myself glumly, she had probably laughed at me worrying and making plans. We were never really partners at all. A little part of me didn't want to believe it, but what else could I think? I ducked back from the window as she rode by. Some friend Maggie had turned out to be.

At dessert that night my dad said, "So Maggie's finally moving, eh, Cyril?"

I nodded.

"In the nick of time, too," said my mom. "I'm glad *we* don't have to pack and move in four days."

"It's not quite a move across the country," my dad said.

"A move is a move," said my mom.

I just kept on eating. It sounded far away, wherever it was.

"Still," my dad said, "it worked out pretty nicely in the end."

"It's ideal," said my mom. "I hear inside the house is a treat."

"I guess you're glad too, Cyril," said my dad. "Soon they'd have been camping in the park."

I wasn't going to laugh. How could grown-ups be so dumb? I said, "May I please be excused?" and left the table.

I went to school mean and miserable the next day. I kept away from Maggie. Once she caught me peeking and smiled that awful knowing smile, then started talking to someone else. It was funny though. She never talked once about moving. After school I had to go to Maggie's place until my mom got home from work. I sat in her tree house and she rode the bike. We didn't say a word.

By Saturday morning nothing had changed, and in a little while Maggie would be gone forever. I was still on the front steps when the door opened behind me and my dad came out. He stood beside me for a moment, looking over at Maggie's while he zipped his jacket up. "Well, Cyril," he said, "it just goes to show you: the more things change, the more they stay the same." He went off to the garage, whistling.

I didn't know what he meant and right then I didn't care. Maggie had just come outside and gone into her garage. I grabbed my tennis ball off the porch and tried to look as if I was having a great time bouncing it off the steps. It worked for a minute, but then I bounced it too high and the ball sailed over my head, thumped off the car, and rolled along Greenapple Street toward Maggie's house, just as Maggie came out of the garage pushing the bike. I froze.

The ball stopped at the end of Maggie's driveway. Maggie looked at the ball, then at me. Now I was stuck. Slowly I walked over, pretending I was very interested in something up in a tree. I was half scared Maggie would do something and half scared she wouldn't. I got the ball and picked it up. Nothing happened. I turned and walked back toward my house. Still nothing happened. Then there was the sound of bike tires on Greenapple Street and Maggie pulled up beside me. We stopped.

I didn't know what to do but Maggie didn't seem to notice. Instead she said, "Cyril, I have decided to give you a break, just to prove that I am a nice person as well as a genius. Even though you have been a complete bozo this week."

I started to get mad when she called me a bozo, but Maggie held up her hand. "We have a deal about this bike, and next week is still my turn to have it. But since I am moving I am going to let you keep the bike right now and use it until whenever I call you and ask for it again. Even though we were sharing it practically all the time until you turned into a sucky-baby."

"What?" I said. "I am not a sucky-baby!"

"Is it a deal or not? I'm doing you a big favour here."

Now I was all mixed up. It looked as if Maggie was going to be nice to me after all.

"Think of it as your last deal with me as the Greenapple Street Genius."

"Okay. . .I guess."

"Good," said Maggie. "It's okay, you don't have to thank me."

We shook hands one last time. Maggie got off the bike and gave it to me to hold up. "Remember," she said, "it's all yours until I call, no matter how long." She looked up the street. I could see her parents getting in the car. "Well, said Maggie, "I better go now. See you, Cyril." She turned and walked away up Greenapple Street.

I felt bad and mixed up watching her go. I should have known Maggie would do something nice for me, I thought, and all I did was get mad at her. After all, it wasn't her fault she had to move. I wished I had something I could give to her, like a trade for the bike. Then I remembered the secret about the Junior Partner.

"Maggieeee," I tried to call, but a lump had got into my throat and nothing came out. Maggie climbed into the car and the chance was gone. The truck engine roared, the car started up and pulled away along Greenapple Street. I thought I saw the flash of a hand at the back window and I raised my own to wave back, then the car turned the corner and Maggie was gone. I looked at her house. Already it seemed cold and empty, scary almost. Without curtains the windows were just black holes. The lawn was covered with dead leaves. It was as if nobody had ever lived there at all.

I swung my leg over the seat of the bike and sat for a minute. It was my bike now, I guessed, but that didn't make me any happier. Finally I got back off and wheeled the bike home. I just didn't feel like riding right then.

As I put the bike in the garage my dad said, "Riding over?" "For now," I said. He looked bewildered as I walked away.

I went in the house and climbed up the stairs to my room. I didn't know what I wanted to do. I flopped on my bed and tried to read a book but it wasn't any fun, so I ended up just staring out the window. Now that the leaves had fallen you could see across the back yards to Maple Avenue. From my window I picked out the big house for sale over there, just a little way down. There were other houses in the way but I could see the very end of the driveway, a bit of the lawn with the sign and the bedroom windows at the top of the house.

Maybe whoever bought Maggie's place will go by there and want that house instead, I thought. Would that mean that Maggie would come back and stay sometimes? Except it was already too late. As I moved my head I saw the front of a big truck parked backwards in the driveway. I twisted back to look at the sign and sure enough, there was a big orange Sold sticker on it. "Rats," I said, and slid down to the floor.

The phone started ringing but I didn't bother to

run for it. I didn't even listen when my mom answered it, just slid lower till I was flat on my back, with only my head propped up on the wall. I stared at my toes.

"Cyril," my mom's voice came up the stairs, "telephone."

"Commm-innnng," I called back and thumped down the stairs.

"Phone's on the table," said my mom when I got to the kitchen. She started down into the basement with a load of laundry.

I picked up the receiver. "Hello?" I said.

A familiar voice answered, "Okay, Cyril, I want the bike now."

"What?" I said. My heart thumped. "Maggie?"

"Who did you think it was? Now don't waste time. The bike, Cyril. The deal. You got the bike till I called for it. So I'm calling. Bring it over."

I was squeezing the phone so tight my hands hurt. "Wh-what—" I said. "But—what—but you— WHERE ARE YOU?"

"Cyrullll," Maggie said, "I'm at my new house. Where else would I be?"

"But WHERE?" I yelled, jumping up and down.

"Go look out your window," said Maggie.

I took the stairs two at a time. A tremendous guess was leaping inside of me. I tore over to the window knowing just where to look. Sure enough a hand was sticking out of a bedroom window holding a cardboard sign. I could just read the words Hi, Cyril printed on it in red. Maggie had moved to Maple Avenue!

"Alllll riiiiiight," I roared and started waving and jumping around in the window. Then I charged back down to the phone. "You moved to Maple Avenue," I yelled, panting and laughing at the same time.

Maggie said, "Of course, silly."

"But why didn't you tell me?"

"I started to, but you got all mad and ran away. Then when you wouldn't talk to me I guessed you didn't know, so I decided to surprise you. And besides, you were being jerky."

"Sorry."

"That's okay."

"Now you can still be the Greenapple Street Genius," I said, "and we can still be partners."

"Partners for sure," Maggie said, "but I'm not the Greenapple Street Genius any more. Now I'm the Maple Avenue Marvel."

The Maple Avenue Marvel; I could get used to that, I thought.

"Hey, know what?" Maggie said. *"You* can be the Greenapple Street Genius. The Maple Avenue Marvel and the Greenapple Street Genius."

"But I'm not a genius."

"That's okay. Nobody will know if you don't tell them. Anyway, you're smart sometimes."

I thought about the moustache problem. And making Maggie write down our deal about the bike. Maybe I *was* kind of smart, sometimes. "Okay," I said.

"Good," said Maggie. "Now ask your mom can you come over to help and stay for lunch too. And don't forget the bike."

"But I just got it," I complained. "I haven't even ridden it yet and you had it all last week."

"That's not my fault. We made a deal, remember?"

"Yeah," I sighed. Maggie had fooled me again. I felt dumb all over again. Then I had my first idea as the Greenapple Street Genius. "Hey, Maggie," I said, "remember our deal about if I found out if the Junior Partner was going to be a boy or a girl? How I get the bike for an extra week? Well. . . ."

"Well, what?" said Maggie, very fast.

"Welllll," I said. "Oh, never mind for now. I'll ask if I can come over. See you."

I hung up the phone. I'd tell her about the Junior Partners later, I decided, just about the time she wanted the bike. Things were changing for the better. Maybe this Greenapple Street Genius wasn't so dumb after all.

More Good Books

Maggie and Me
Ted Staunton

Poor Cyril! Without Maggie life would be a lot easier, but it would also be a lot more boring. MAGGIE AND ME — a collection of five funny stories starring Cyril and his best friend Maggie, the Greenapple Street Genius. No matter what they do, they seem to be in trouble.

Ted Staunton wanted to be a cowboy when he was small, but somehow he became a writer instead. He is also a musician and will perform his songs for anyone who wants to listen. The author of *Puddleman*, *Taking Care of Crumley* (also starring Cyril and Maggie) and *Simon's Surprise*, he is married and lives in Toronto.

Kids Can Press

More Good Books

Guppy Love, Or, The Day the Fish Tank Exploded
Frank O'Keefe

School began with a bang. It started the day the fish tank exploded, and before it was over there was an attack of "killer" bees, a burglary and a fire. And Natalie was in the thick of it — with a terrific crush.

"I've heard about women falling in love with older men. I've sneaked a look at some of the paperbacks my mother sometimes reads. Often they have women in their twenties falling in love with men over forty — real mushy stuff — but this was ridiculous! I'm only in Grade 5. Who ever heard of a 10-year-old, going on eleven, falling in love with her teacher who is really old — at least thirty-five, maybe more.''

Kids Can Press

More Good Books

Could Dracula Live in Woodford?
Mary Howarth

Gulping, Jennie leaned into the doorway and tried to see into the darkness. "I can't see anything," she whispered.

Go in a few steps, I'm not making it up.

Jennie looked anxiously at Beth. "Will you come with me?"

She nodded. Holding hands, they stepped over the threshold into the silent house. In the dim light, from a far wall, two enormous eyes stared at them — dead eyes — expressionless and unblinking.

Kids Can Press